Liar, Liar,
Pants on Fire

Liar, Liar,
Pants on Fire

Diane deGroat

chronicle books · san francisco

Typeset in Korinna.
The illustrations in this book were rendered in watercolor.
Manufactured in China.
ISBN-10 0-8118-5453-1
ISBN-13 978-0-8118-5453-5

The Library of Congress has catalogued the previous edition as follows:
De Groat, Diane.
Liar, liar, pants on fire / Diane deGroat.
p. cm.
Summary: Gilbert is nervous about portraying George Washington in front of the class, and he feels even worse
when he cannot find his main prop.
ISBN 1-58717-214-3 (alk. paper) — ISBN 1-58717-215-1 (lib. bdg. : alk. paper)
[1. Schools—Fiction. 2. Theater—Fiction. 3. Self-confidence—Fiction. 4. Honesty—Fiction.] l. Title.
PZ7.D3639 Li 2003
[E]—dc21
2002015496

Distributed in Canada by Raincoast Books
9050 Shaughnessy Street, Vancouver, British Columbia V6P 6E5

10 9 8 7 6 5 4 3 2 1

Chronicle Books LLC
85 Second Street, San Francisco, California 94105

www.chroniclekids.com

I cannot tell a lie—
four heads are better than one.
Thank you to Sean, Amanda, and Norm
for your input.
—D. D.

Gilbert was having a bad day. His class had been reading stories about famous people, and now Mrs. Byrd wanted them to make up plays to show what they had learned. Gilbert didn't want to be in a play. He was sure he would get nervous and make a mistake.

Even worse, Mrs. Byrd stuck him in a group with know-it-all Philip and bossy Margaret.

"Let's do a play about George Washington and the cherry tree," Philip suggested.

"O.K.," said Margaret. "I'll be George Washington."

"I should be the president," Philip said, "because I'm the best student in the class."

"I said it first!" Margaret insisted.

Gilbert just wanted to be the cherry tree so he wouldn't have any lines.

Mrs. Byrd settled it by writing the parts on slips of paper and having them each pick one. To his surprise, Gilbert picked George Washington. Margaret picked George's father. And Philip was the cherry tree.

Mrs. Byrd opened a big box of costumes. "You can practice your plays now and share them with the class tomorrow," she said.

She gave Lewis a tall black hat for his role as Abraham Lincoln. Patty wanted to be Sally Ride, so she got a motorcycle helmet that looked just like part of a space suit.

Mrs. Byrd handed Gilbert a three-cornered hat. When Gilbert put it on, he felt better. Maybe he would be a good George Washington after all.

During practice, Gilbert pretended to chop trees for firewood. Then he chopped at Philip's leg. Philip said "ow" and dropped to the floor.

Margaret came up to Gilbert and said, "Oh, no! My favorite little cherry tree has been chopped down. Tell me who has done this horrible thing?"

Gilbert held up his paper ax and said, "Uh . . . me?"

"That's not the way it was in the book," Philip said. "You're supposed to say, 'I cannot tell a lie. I cut down your cherry tree. I am sorry.'"

Margaret added, "Then I say, 'Because you told the truth, I will not punish you.'"

Philip sighed. "I still think I should be George Washington."

For the rest of the day, Gilbert practiced his lines. At
lunch Patty asked him what kind of sandwich he had, and
Gilbert replied, "I cannot tell a lie. It is peanut butter and
jelly!"

During arithmetic, Mrs. Byrd asked him to add six and
six. Gilbert said, "I cannot tell a lie. The answer is twelve!"

Gilbert wanted to practice at home, too—with the hat.
When no one was looking, he slipped it into his book bag.

Gilbert wore the hat to the supper table and announced, "I cannot tell a lie. I'm starving!"

His sister Lola said, "Me, too!"

"Try this soup," Mother said, passing the bowl. "It's a new recipe."

Gilbert took a spoonful and said, "I cannot tell a lie. I don't like it."

Lola put her spoon down and said, "Yucky soup!"

Then Gilbert said, "I cannot tell a lie. Lola is a big copycat!"

Lola started to cry, and Mother said, "That's enough, Gilbert."

"But it's the truth," Gilbert said.

Mother sighed and said, "Sometimes it's better to say nothing than to hurt people's feelings."

Gilbert groaned. It was hard being George Washington!

Before getting ready for bed, Gilbert carefully tucked the hat into his backpack, so he could take it back to school in the morning. He didn't want Mrs. Byrd to notice it was gone. He took a bath and brushed his teeth, repeating his lines over and over so he wouldn't forget them.

When Gilbert walked to school with Patty the next morning he said, "I've been practicing my part, but I'm still nervous about making a mistake. I just know that bully Lewis is going to laugh at me."

"I promise not to laugh if you make a mistake,"
Patty said.

And Gilbert said, "I cannot tell a lie, Patty. You are a
good friend!"

When it was time to get ready for the play, Gilbert
opened his backpack and reached inside. He felt his
spelling book and his notebook, but he didn't feel his
three-cornered hat. It was gone!

Just then Margaret asked, "Where's your hat, Gilbert?
It's not in the box."

Gilbert said quickly, "I didn't take it!"

Margaret said, "I bet Philip took it. He wanted to be
George Washington."

"Philip!" Gilbert said. If it wasn't in his backpack,
someone must have taken it, and it must have been Philip!

"But I didn't take it," Philip said.

"Liar!" Margaret shouted.

"Liar, liar, pants on fire!" Gilbert sang.

Lewis heard him and asked, "What's on fire?"

Frank said, "There's a fire?"

Patty ran to Mrs. Byrd, shouting, "The school's on fire!"

Mrs. Byrd said, "I didn't hear the fire alarm."

"But that's what Frank said," Patty replied. "It must be true!"

"I heard it from Lewis," Frank said.

"I heard it from Gilbert," said Lewis. "He said something was on fire!"

Gilbert sighed. "All I said was 'liar, liar, pants on fire.'"
And Philip shouted, "I DID NOT TAKE GEORGE
WASHINGTON'S HAT!"

Mrs. Byrd opened a shopping bag. "Here's the hat, Gilbert. Your mother just brought it in. You know you weren't supposed to take it home."

"Oops," Gilbert said, turning red. "I was going to bring it back."

Margaret pointed her finger. "You lied about taking the hat, Gilbert. Philip almost got in trouble!"

Gilbert turned to Philip and handed him the hat. "I'm sorry," he said. "You were right. I'm not a very good George Washington. You should have the part."

But Philip handed it back, saying, "It's O.K., Gilbert. You said you were sorry. Just like Washington."

"My beard itches," Lewis complained. "Are we going to do our plays or not?"

As each group did their play, Gilbert grew more and more nervous. When Patty-the-Astronaut tripped over her space boots, Lewis and some of the other kids laughed. Gilbert didn't laugh. He knew he might mess up, too.

But when it was Gilbert's turn, he said his lines
without a single mistake.

And that's the truth.